SHOCK VALUE presents
THE DISEASE

written by Paul Kane
art by Pawel Kardis
lettering by Nikki Foxrobot

introduction by Mark Alan Miller

Hellbound Media Editors:
Mark Adams and Matt Warner

Patient Zero:
Amy Cummins

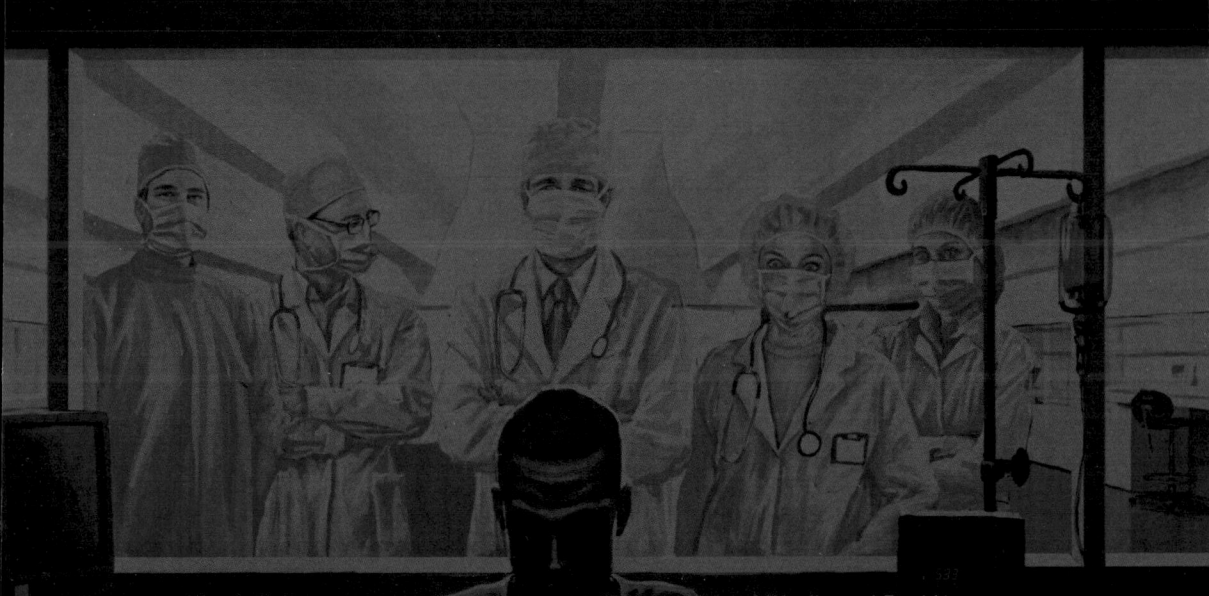

Shock Value presents... The Disease (c) 2016 Hellbound Media and Paul Kane
Published by Hellbound Media. All prominent characters are trademarks of Hellbound Media and their creators. The events and characters in this book are entirely fictional. Any similarity to actual persons, living or dead, is coincidental. With the exception of artwork used for review purposes, no portion of this book may be reproduced, by any means, without the written permission of the copyright holder.

Introduction
Not-So-Subtle Bodies

Horror wears all forms. The supernatural. The paranormal. Horror in the woods. Horror in the suburbs. For every metaphor that we can put a fear to, there is a sub-genre of horror that has tackled it, and shed a light on our deepest, darkest terrors. Paul Kane's The Disease is pure body horror, and a shining, powerfully written example of the truth each sub-genre is capable of telling.

We can level the woods, and there wouldn't be anything left to fear lurking behind the trees. We can demolish the suburbs, and in living our lives free from the ever oppressive white-picket-fence, the robotic smile of the Stepford metaphor would cease to be. But as long as we write, and breathe, and squirm on this planet, body horror will stand.

What's not to fear about the body? It's soft, and easily penetrated. It bleeds. It feels pain. It betrays us. When it meets other bodies with viruses, it gets sick. It needs sleep. And that's just the everyday stuff of being. We can change our bodies – make them bigger or smaller as an act of sheer will, or an incredible act of denial, psyche depending. We can become prisoners in our own bodies, too. Accidents leave us paralyzed, but with our minds fully aware of all that is happening.

In the end, our bodies are what fail us, and we must leave them. And, of course, whatever happens after that is anyone's guess. But the body stubbornly gives out anyway. In refusing to answer any of life's great mysteries, the body becomes responsible for the big questions. Why are we here? Where do we go when we're not here anymore? If the body was impenetrable, we'd never have need for these questions.

But alas, like so much meat, we spoil. Our bodies give in to the gravity of time. They protest and turn against us when we've done nothing to deserve it except live long enough to be punished for it. The Disease understands this treachery, and explores it fearlessly. What happens when the body betrays you? What happens when nobody can tell you what's wrong? Why is this happening to you? What kind of God would allow this farce to continue to play out?

And, like all great stories, the answer comes from a place of understanding the power of metaphor. The body, as it turns out, has little to do with the individual. And when the story plays out its final turn, what we're left with is something that makes so much sense it only gives way to more terror. That, my friends, is horror.

I hope you enjoy reading and re-reading The Disease as much as I did. And by that regard, with every subsequent reading, I sincerely hope its resonance diminishes.

Mark Alan Miller

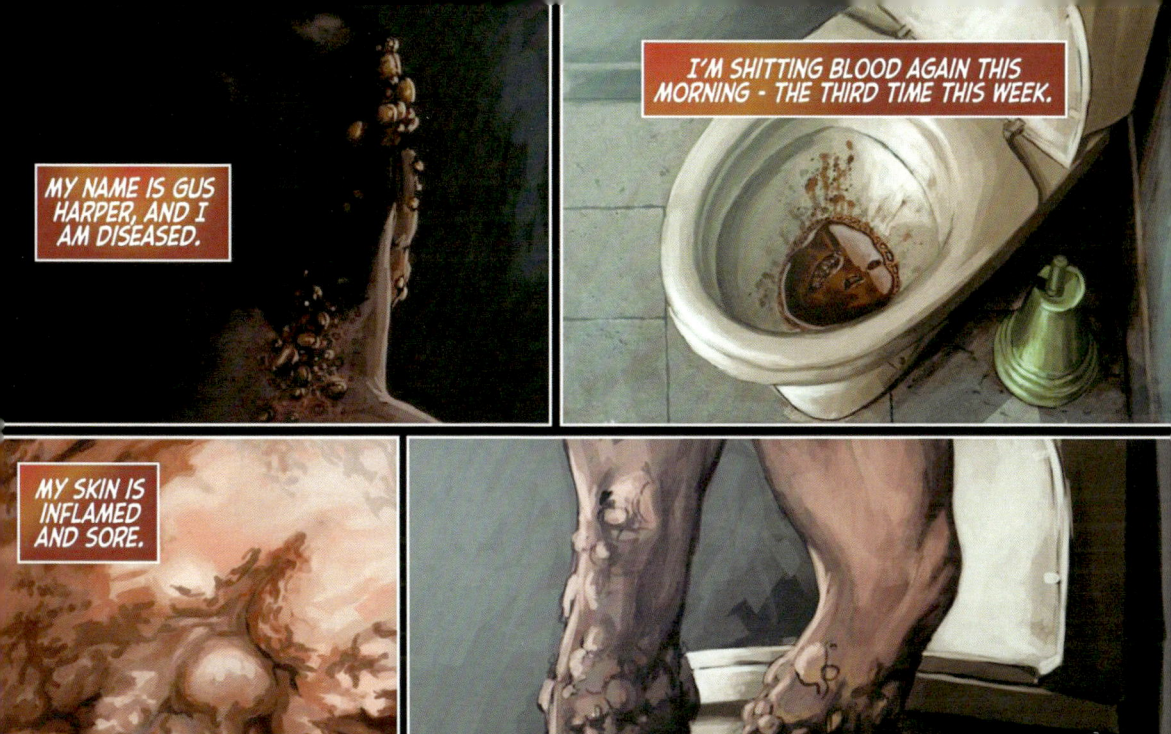

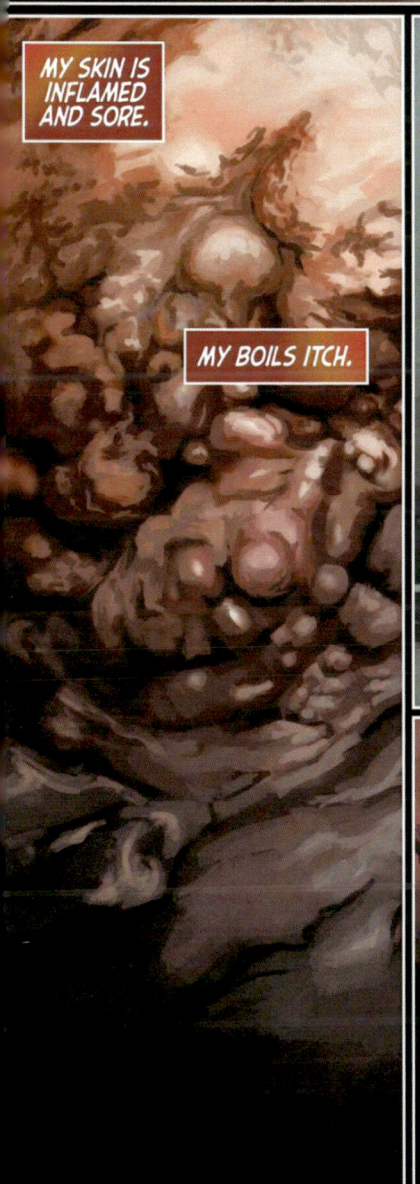

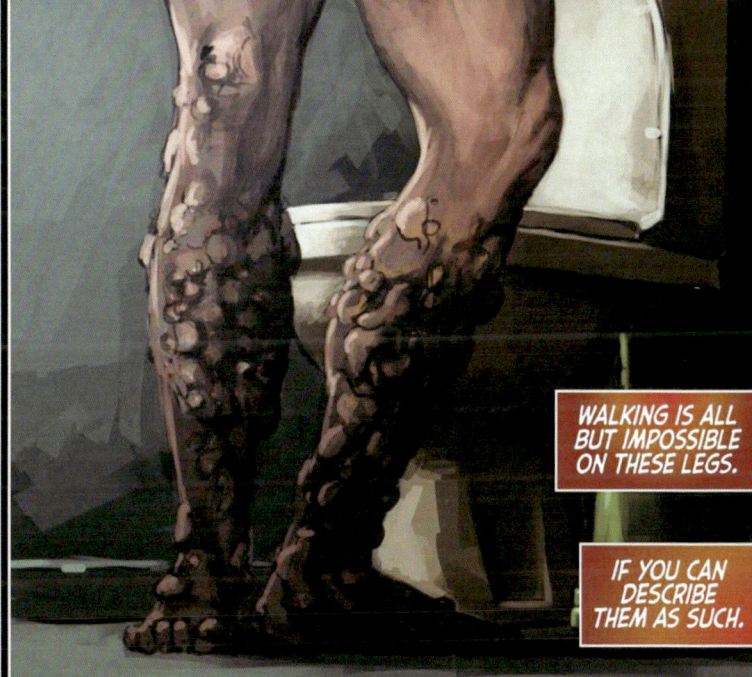

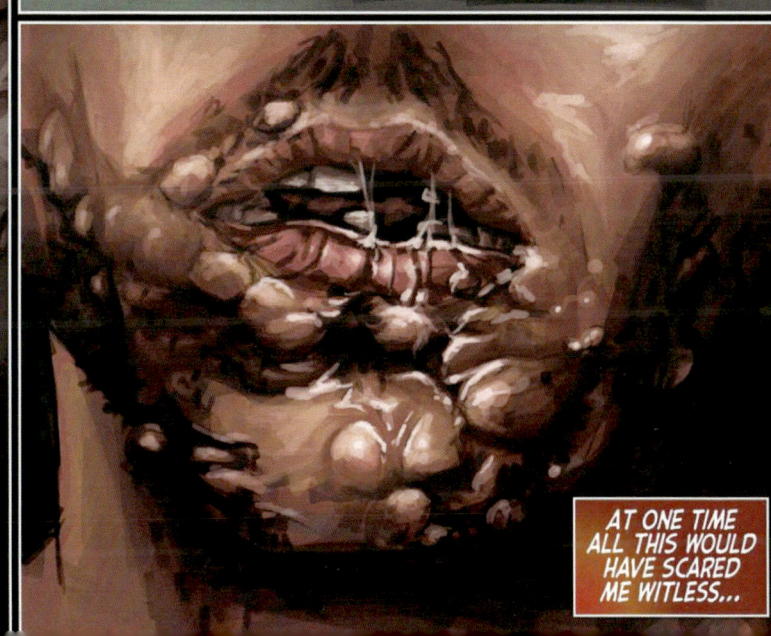

MY NAME IS GUS HARPER, AND I AM DISEASED.

I'M SHITTING BLOOD AGAIN THIS MORNING - THE THIRD TIME THIS WEEK.

MY SKIN IS INFLAMED AND SORE.

MY BOILS ITCH.

WALKING IS ALL BUT IMPOSSIBLE ON THESE LEGS.

IF YOU CAN DESCRIBE THEM AS SUCH.

AT ONE TIME ALL THIS WOULD HAVE SCARED ME WITLESS...

NOT ANY MORE.

I'VE SEEN TOO MUCH; GONE THROUGH TOO MUCH.

THE MEMORIES ARE STILL ALIVE, TRAPPED IN WHAT'S LEFT OF MY MIND.

BUT HOW LONG THEY'LL REMAIN THERE NOW IS ANYONE'S GUESS.

THE DISEASE

I REMEMBER THE MORNING IT CAME ON.
A SATURDAY IN LATE JANUARY.
AND I REMEMBER THE DREAM.
MAINLY BECAUSE I'M STILL HAVING IT.
A DREAM OF BLUENESS, SO BRIGHT IT ALMOST BLINDS ME.
I ALWAYS WAKE JUST BEFORE MAKING CONTACT.
ON THAT PARTICULAR MORNING I WOKE UP NEXT TO RACHEL.
AND I WATCHED HER SLEEPING.
THE WAY HER SOFT MOUTH OPENED AND CLOSED, EYELIDS FLUTTERING AS SHE DREAMED HER OWN PRIVATE DREAMS.
I SUPPOSE SHE MUST HAVE SENSED ME LOOKING AT HER.
BECAUSE SHE WOKE UP THEN.
WE'D BEEN TOGETHER A YEAR AND A HALF, BUT SHE COULD STILL GET ME GOING.

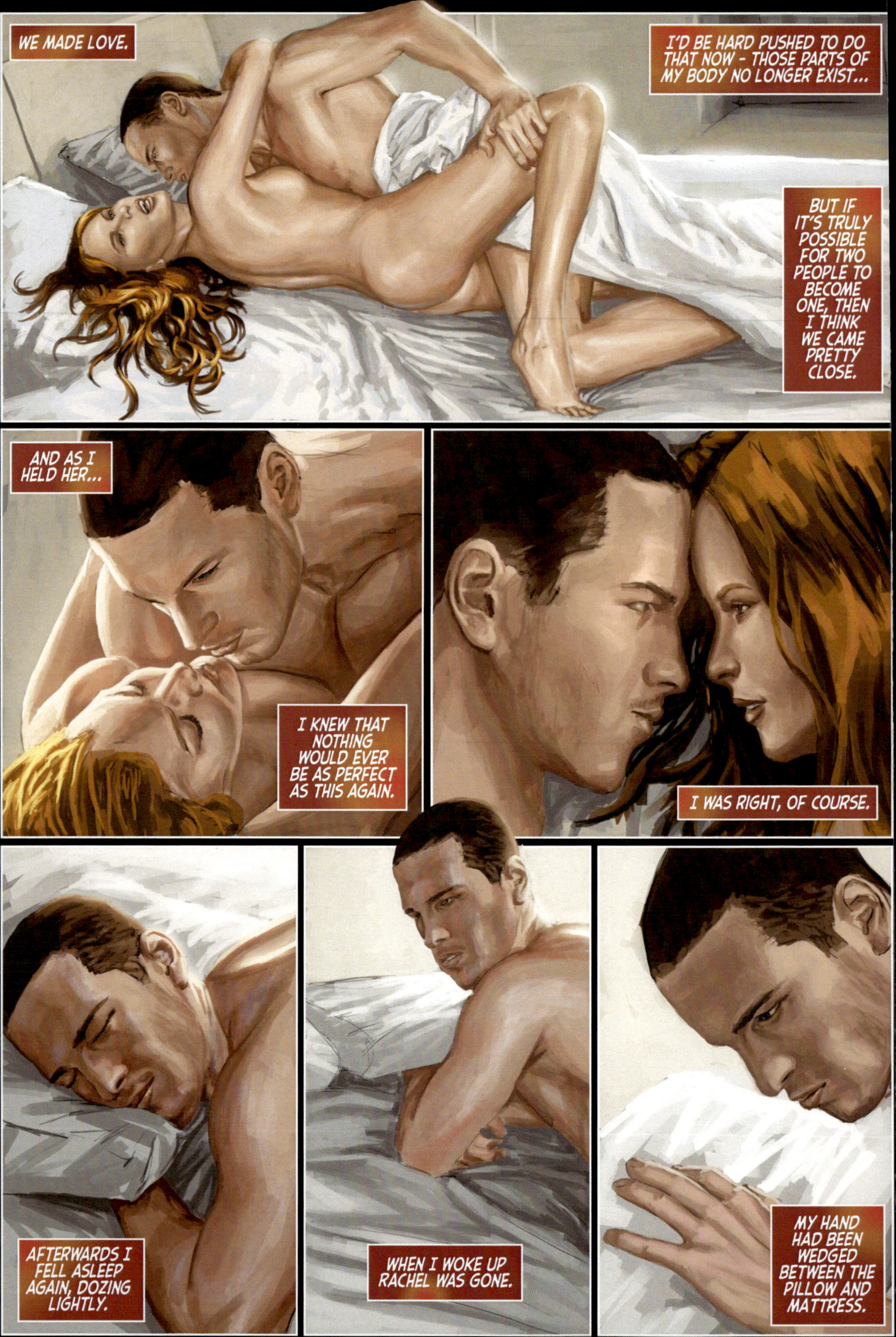
WE MADE LOVE.
I'D BE HARD PUSHED TO DO THAT NOW - THOSE PARTS OF MY BODY NO LONGER EXIST...
BUT IF IT'S TRULY POSSIBLE FOR TWO PEOPLE TO BECOME ONE, THEN I THINK WE CAME PRETTY CLOSE.
AND AS I HELD HER...
I KNEW THAT NOTHING WOULD EVER BE AS PERFECT AS THIS AGAIN.
I WAS RIGHT, OF COURSE.
AFTERWARDS I FELL ASLEEP AGAIN, DOZING LIGHTLY.
WHEN I WOKE UP RACHEL WAS GONE.
MY HAND HAD BEEN WEDGED BETWEEN THE PILLOW AND MATTRESS.

I FELT THE FAMILIAR ONSET OF PINS AND NEEDLES.

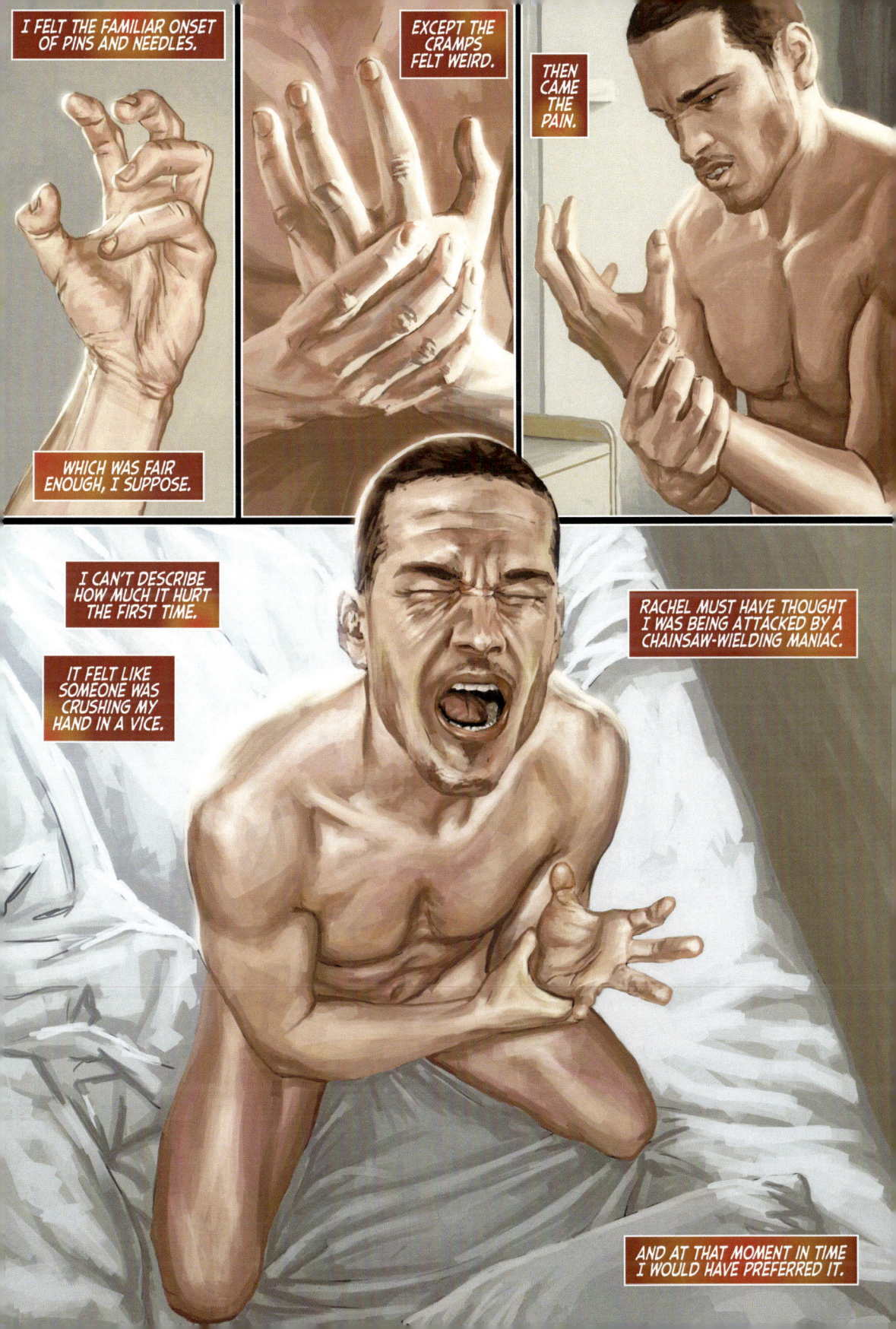

EXCEPT THE CRAMPS FELT WEIRD.

THEN CAME THE PAIN.

WHICH WAS FAIR ENOUGH, I SUPPOSE.

I CAN'T DESCRIBE HOW MUCH IT HURT THE FIRST TIME.

IT FELT LIKE SOMEONE WAS CRUSHING MY HAND IN A VICE.

RACHEL MUST HAVE THOUGHT I WAS BEING ATTACKED BY A CHAINSAW-WIELDING MANIAC.

AND AT THAT MOMENT IN TIME I WOULD HAVE PREFERRED IT.

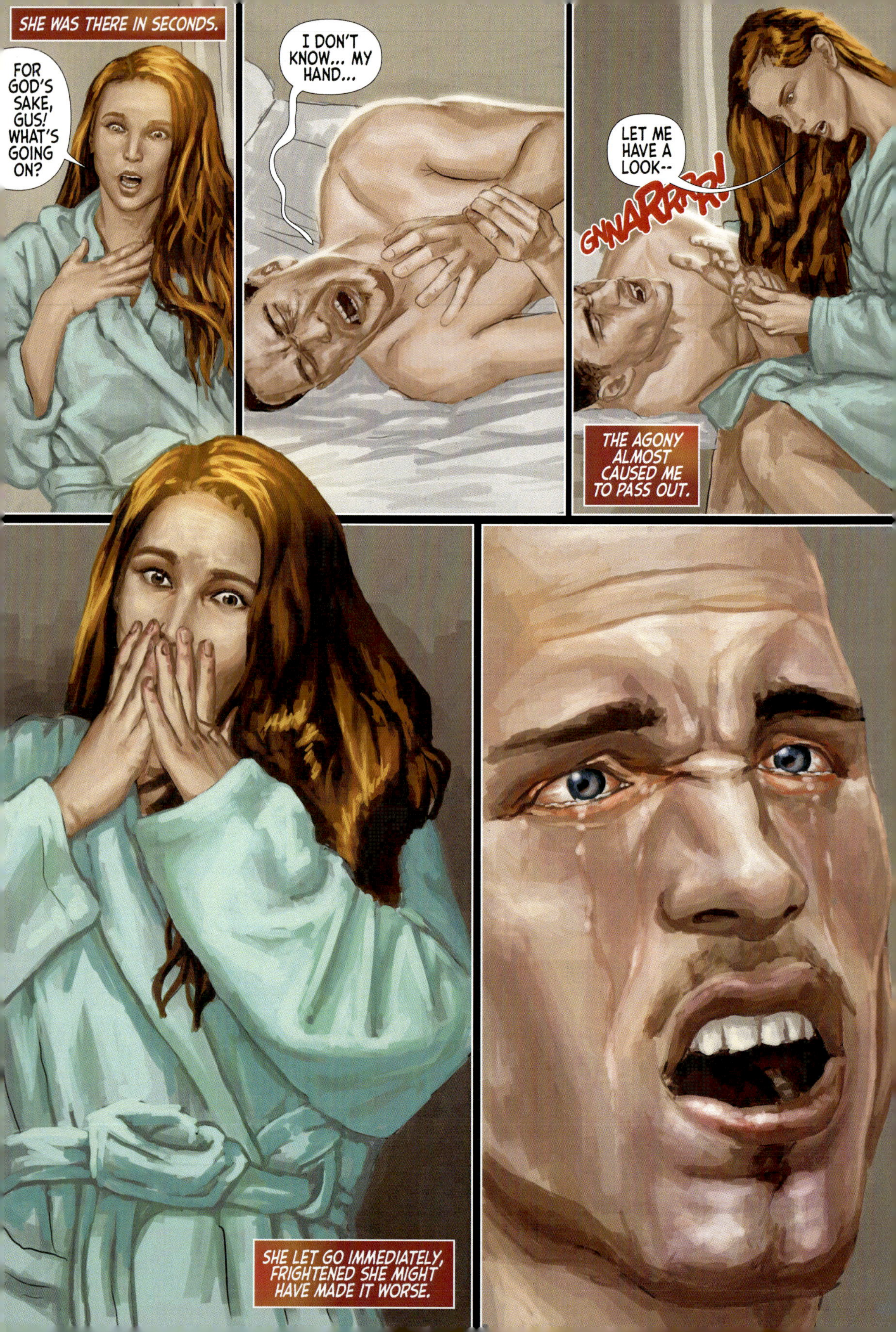
SHE WAS THERE IN SECONDS.
FOR GOD'S SAKE, GUS! WHAT'S GOING ON?
I DON'T KNOW... MY HAND...
LET ME HAVE A LOOK--
GNARRRR!
THE AGONY ALMOST CAUSED ME TO PASS OUT.
SHE LET GO IMMEDIATELY, FRIGHTENED SHE MIGHT HAVE MADE IT WORSE.

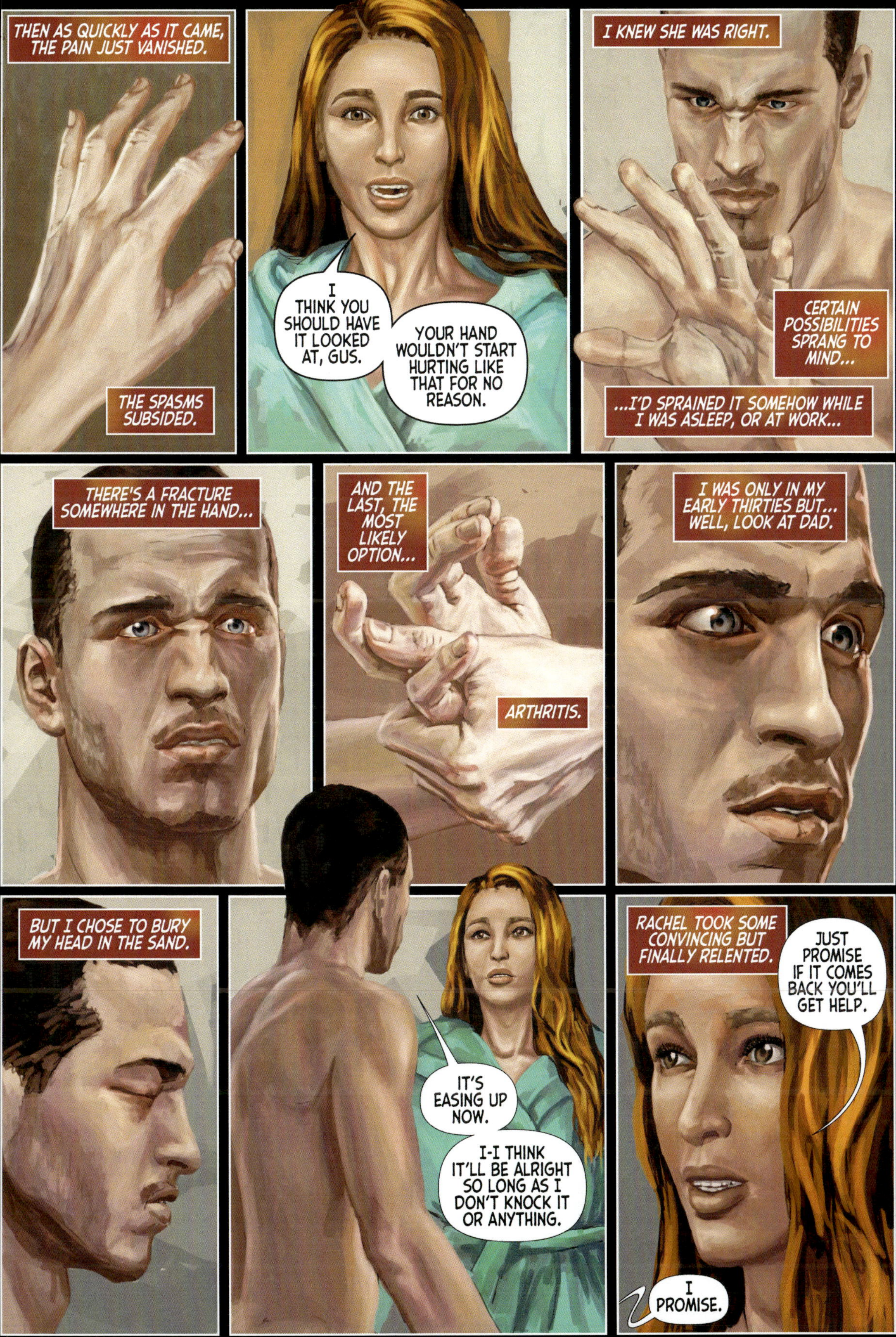
THEN AS QUICKLY AS IT CAME, THE PAIN JUST VANISHED.
THE SPASMS SUBSIDED.
I THINK YOU SHOULD HAVE IT LOOKED AT, GUS.
YOUR HAND WOULDN'T START HURTING LIKE THAT FOR NO REASON.
I KNEW SHE WAS RIGHT.
CERTAIN POSSIBILITIES SPRANG TO MIND...
...I'D SPRAINED IT SOMEHOW WHILE I WAS ASLEEP, OR AT WORK...
THERE'S A FRACTURE SOMEWHERE IN THE HAND...
AND THE LAST, THE MOST LIKELY OPTION...
ARTHRITIS.
I WAS ONLY IN MY EARLY THIRTIES BUT... WELL, LOOK AT DAD.
BUT I CHOSE TO BURY MY HEAD IN THE SAND.
IT'S EASING UP NOW.
I-I THINK IT'LL BE ALRIGHT SO LONG AS I DON'T KNOCK IT OR ANYTHING.
RACHEL TOOK SOME CONVINCING BUT FINALLY RELENTED.
JUST PROMISE IF IT COMES BACK YOU'LL GET HELP.
I PROMISE.

IT WAS EASY TO KEEP THAT PROMISE FOR A WHILE BECAUSE NOTHING ELSE HAPPENED. I WON'T SAY I FORGOT ALL ABOUT IT, BUT YOU KNOW HOW IT IS...

YOU PRIORITISE.

MY LIFE RETURNED TO NORMAL. I WENT TO WORK, LOSING MYSELF IN THE DAILY GRIND AT THE FACTORY.

I HAD LUNCH IN THE CANTEEN WITH THE LADS AT DINNERTIME.

I WENT BACK HOME FOR NIGHTS IN FRONT OF THE TV WITH RACHEL IN THE EVENING.

CATCHING UP WITH THE STATE OF THE WORLD.

THE USUAL STUFF: GROWING TENSIONS ABROAD.

MURDER, TERRORISM, CHEMICAL POLLUTANTS...

I THINK IT WAS ABOUT MIDWAY THROUGH THE SECOND WEEK THAT IT CAME BACK.
NO WARNING, NO STRANGE NUMBNESS THIS TIME. JUST WHACK!
AND THE PAIN WAS SHOOTING UP MY ARM THIS TIME.
MERCIFULLY, I DID LOSE CONSCIOUSNESS THE SECOND TIME.
WHEN I WOKE, I WAS IN WHAT GRIMWALD'S LAUGHINGLY CALL THEIR INFIRMARY.
I HADN'T HAD CAUSE TO VISIT SINCE THEIR ANNUAL MEDICAL, LAST JULY.
CLEAN BILL OF HEALTH I GOT, TOO. WHAT A JOKE!

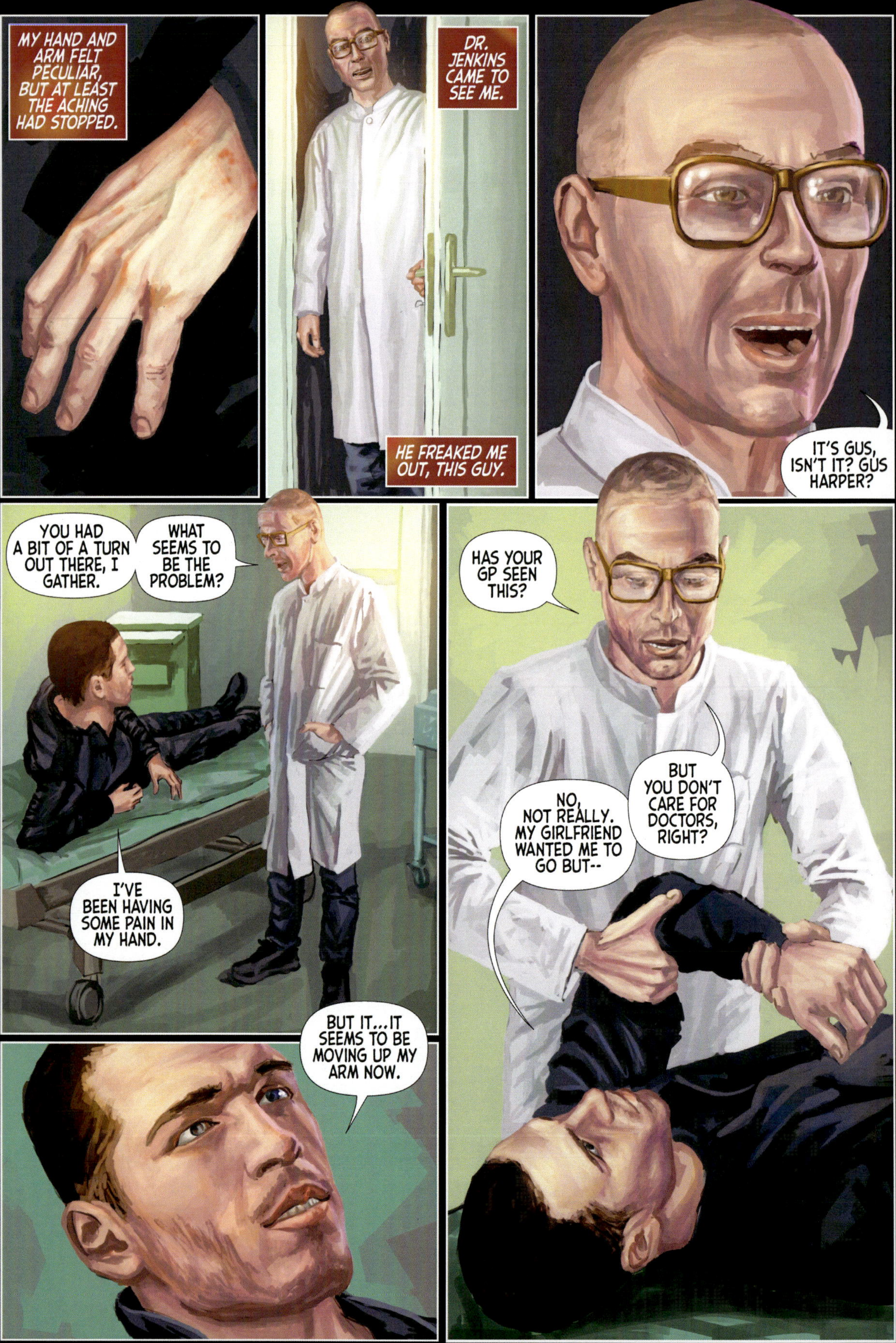
MY HAND AND ARM FELT PECULIAR, BUT AT LEAST THE ACHING HAD STOPPED.
DR. JENKINS CAME TO SEE ME.
HE FREAKED ME OUT, THIS GUY.
IT'S GUS, ISN'T IT? GUS HARPER?
YOU HAD A BIT OF A TURN OUT THERE, I GATHER.
WHAT SEEMS TO BE THE PROBLEM?
I'VE BEEN HAVING SOME PAIN IN MY HAND.
BUT IT...IT SEEMS TO BE MOVING UP MY ARM NOW.
HAS YOUR GP SEEN THIS?
NO, NOT REALLY. MY GIRLFRIEND WANTED ME TO GO BUT--
BUT YOU DON'T CARE FOR DOCTORS, RIGHT?

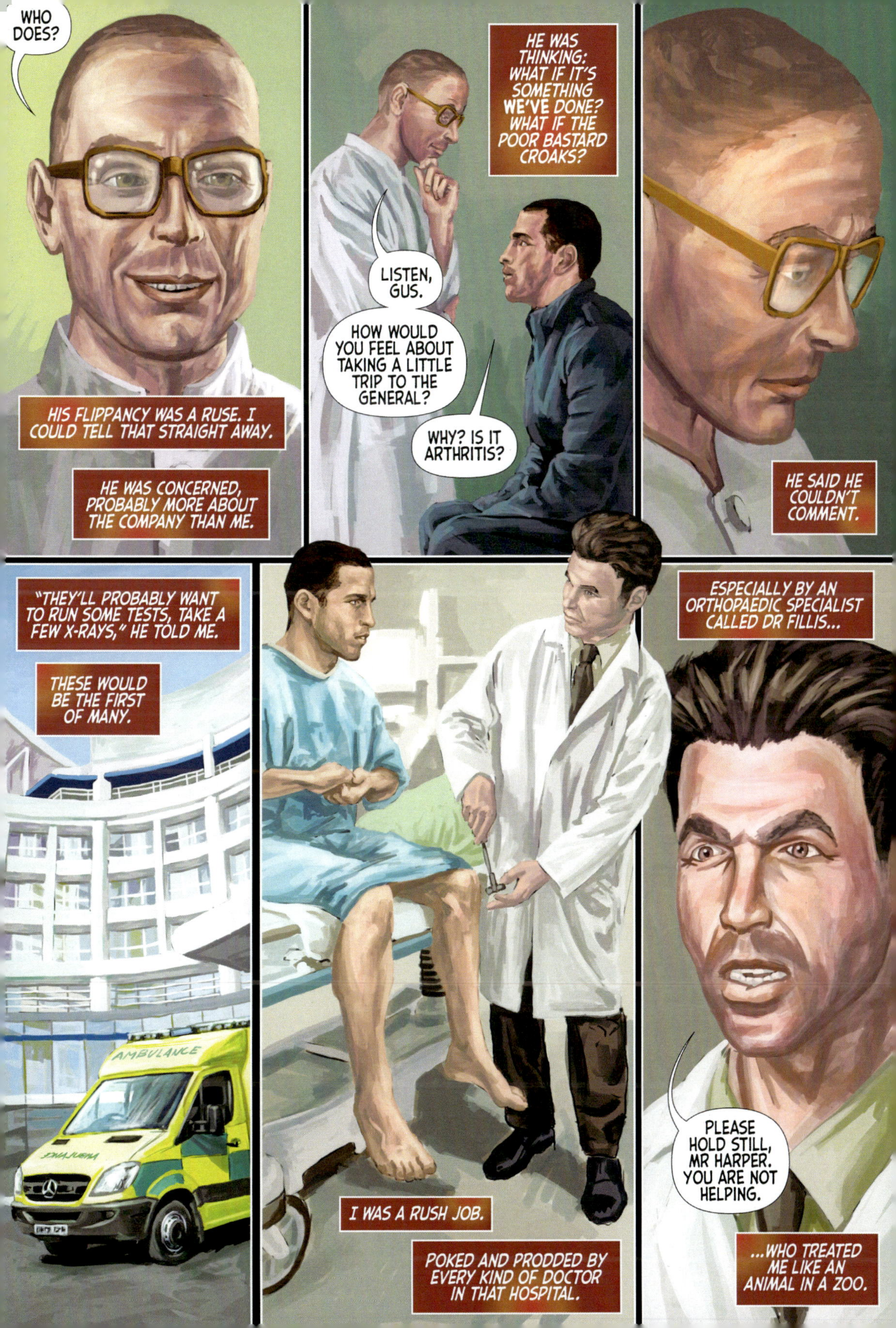
WHO DOES?
HIS FLIPPANCY WAS A RUSE. I COULD TELL THAT STRAIGHT AWAY.
HE WAS CONCERNED, PROBABLY MORE ABOUT THE COMPANY THAN ME.
HE WAS THINKING: WHAT IF IT'S SOMETHING WE'VE DONE? WHAT IF THE POOR BASTARD CROAKS?
LISTEN, GUS.
HOW WOULD YOU FEEL ABOUT TAKING A LITTLE TRIP TO THE GENERAL?
WHY? IS IT ARTHRITIS?
HE SAID HE COULDN'T COMMENT.
"THEY'LL PROBABLY WANT TO RUN SOME TESTS, TAKE A FEW X-RAYS," HE TOLD ME.
THESE WOULD BE THE FIRST OF MANY.
AMBULANCE
I WAS A RUSH JOB.
POKED AND PRODDED BY EVERY KIND OF DOCTOR IN THAT HOSPITAL.
ESPECIALLY BY AN ORTHOPAEDIC SPECIALIST CALLED DR FILLIS...
PLEASE HOLD STILL, MR HARPER. YOU ARE NOT HELPING.
...WHO TREATED ME LIKE AN ANIMAL IN A ZOO.

X-RAYS CONFIRMED THAT IT WASN'T BROKEN.

BUT MORE TESTS WERE NEEDED...

RACHEL CAME TO COLLECT ME AT AROUND HALF FIVE, STRAIGHT FROM WORK.

I DIDN'T SEE THE SENSE IN BOTHERING HER BEFORE THEN.

SHE WAS FULL OF QUESTIONS, THOUGH.

QUESTIONS I COULDN'T ANSWER.

ALL I COULD TELL HER WAS WHAT THEY'D TOLD ME...

THAT THEY WOULD KNOW MORE IN A FEW DAYS WHEN THE TEST RESULTS CAME BACK.

MEANWHILE I WAS STUCK AT HOME ON THE SICK.

BUT FILLIS HAD PRESCRIBED SOME ANTI-INFLAMMATORIES AND PAINKILLERS.

I BEGAN VOMITING A COUPLE OF TIMES A DAY.

I THOUGHT IT WAS A SIDE-EFFECT OF THE DRUGS.

BUT NOW I'M NOT SO SURE.

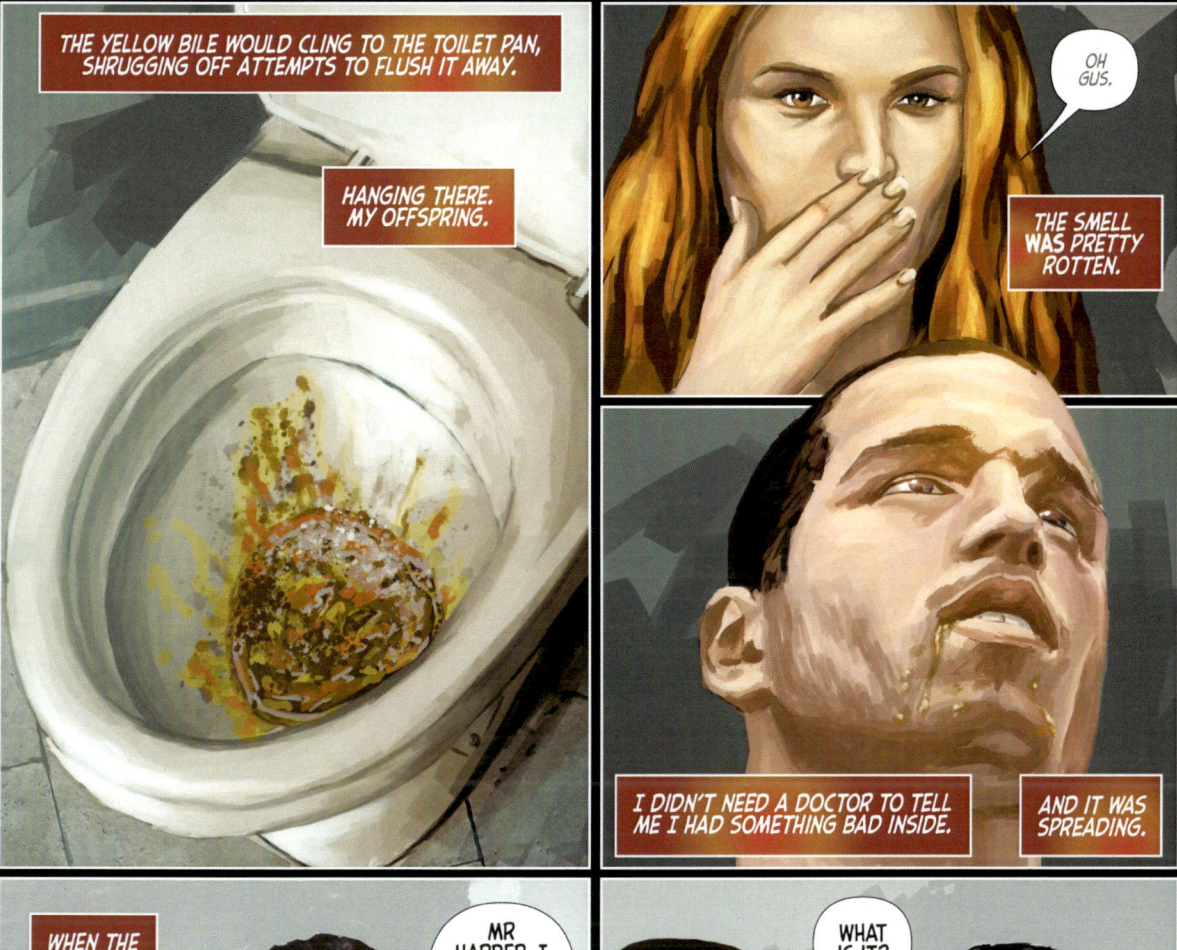

THE YELLOW BILE WOULD CLING TO THE TOILET PAN, SHRUGGING OFF ATTEMPTS TO FLUSH IT AWAY.

HANGING THERE. MY OFFSPRING.

OH, GUS.

THE SMELL WAS PRETTY ROTTEN.

I DIDN'T NEED A DOCTOR TO TELL ME I HAD SOMETHING BAD INSIDE.

AND IT WAS SPREADING.

WHEN THE RESULTS CAME IN, FILLIS CALLED ME BACK.

MR HARPER, I HAVE SOME RATHER PERPLEXING NEWS.

WHAT IS IT?

THERE'S NO EASY WAY TO SAY THIS...

...WE SIMPLY DON'T *KNOW* WHAT'S WRONG.

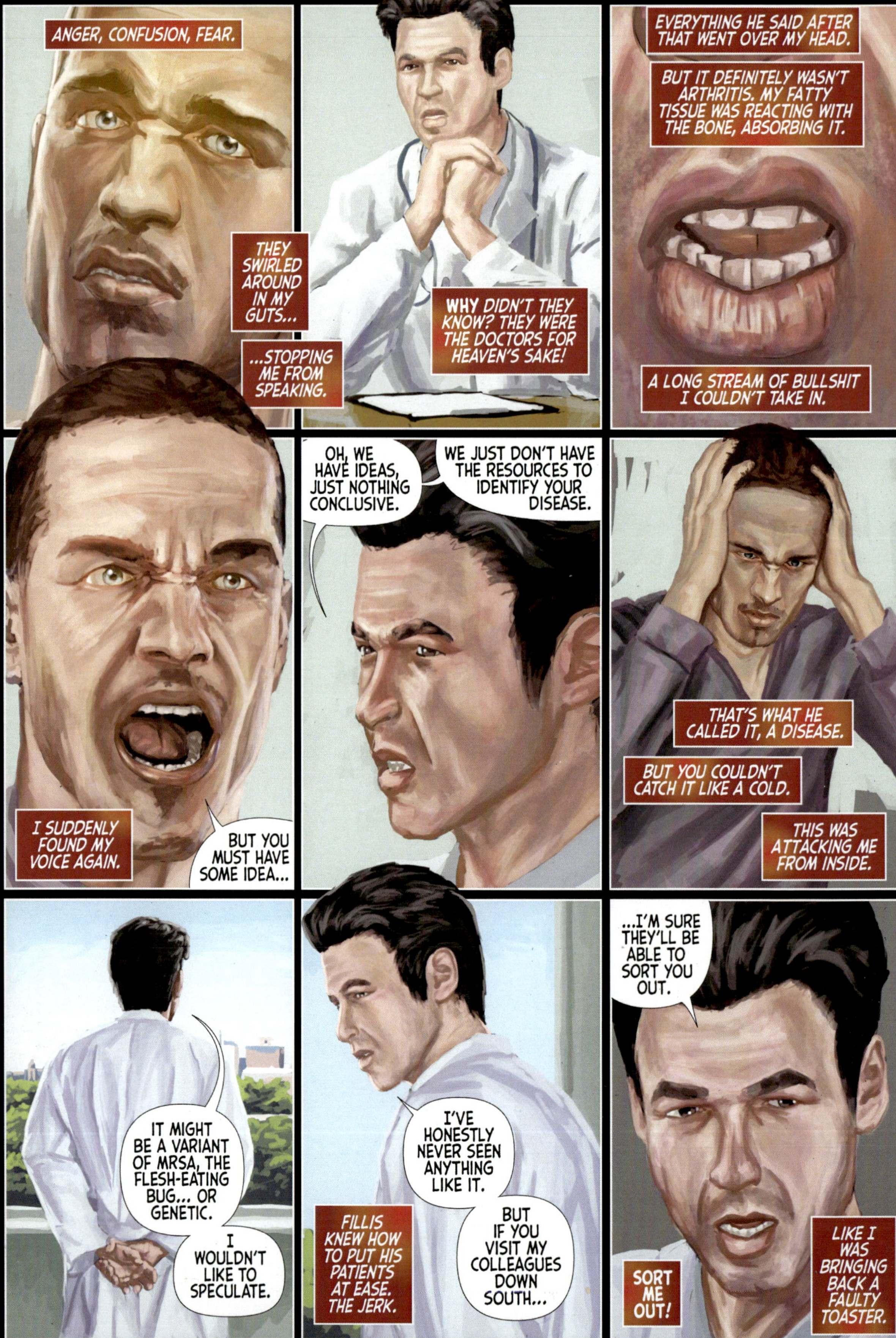
ANGER, CONFUSION, FEAR.
THEY SWIRLED AROUND IN MY GUTS...
...STOPPING ME FROM SPEAKING.
WHY DIDN'T THEY KNOW? THEY WERE THE DOCTORS FOR HEAVEN'S SAKE!
EVERYTHING HE SAID AFTER THAT WENT OVER MY HEAD.
BUT IT DEFINITELY WASN'T ARTHRITIS. MY FATTY TISSUE WAS REACTING WITH THE BONE, ABSORBING IT.
A LONG STREAM OF BULLSHIT I COULDN'T TAKE IN.
I SUDDENLY FOUND MY VOICE AGAIN.
BUT YOU MUST HAVE SOME IDEA...
OH, WE HAVE IDEAS, JUST NOTHING CONCLUSIVE.
WE JUST DON'T HAVE THE RESOURCES TO IDENTIFY YOUR DISEASE.
THAT'S WHAT HE CALLED IT, A DISEASE.
BUT YOU COULDN'T CATCH IT LIKE A COLD.
THIS WAS ATTACKING ME FROM INSIDE.
IT MIGHT BE A VARIANT OF MRSA, THE FLESH-EATING BUG... OR GENETIC.
I WOULDN'T LIKE TO SPECULATE.
I'VE HONESTLY NEVER SEEN ANYTHING LIKE IT.
BUT IF YOU VISIT MY COLLEAGUES DOWN SOUTH...
FILLIS KNEW HOW TO PUT HIS PATIENTS AT EASE. THE JERK.
...I'M SURE THEY'LL BE ABLE TO SORT YOU OUT.
SORT ME OUT!
LIKE I WAS BRINGING BACK A FAULTY TOASTER.

MORE TESTS, MORE WAITING. I DIDN'T RELISH IT.
BUT RACHEL WAS INSISTENT.
YOU'RE GOING. IF NOT FOR YOUR OWN SAKE THEN FOR MINE.
I HAVEN'T SLEPT IN A WEEK.
SHE TOOK TIME OFF, PROBABLY TO MAKE SURE I ACTUALLY WENT.
MY 'TREATMENT' WAS FREE. I WAS, AFTER ALL... A SPECIAL CASE.
SOMEONE WAS EVEN WRITING A PAPER ON ME.
YEAH, FUCKING HARPER'S DISEASE. ROLL UP, ROLL UP!
THE INSTITUTE ITSELF WAS LIKE SOMETHING FROM THE FUTURE.
SO MANY DOCTORS, THEIR FACES BLURRED INTO ONE, THEIR NAMES A MISHMASH.
THEY DID EVERYTHING BAR TURN ME INSIDE OUT.
AND THEY WOULD'VE TOO, IF I'D SIGNED THE RIGHT CONSENT FORMS.
BIOPSIES WERE TAKEN, SAMPLES GALORE...
URINE, STOOLS, SKIN, BLOOD... EVEN SEMEN! AND PHOTOGRAPHS RECORDED THE ONSLAUGHT.

RACHEL WAS INCREDIBLY SUPPORTIVE.

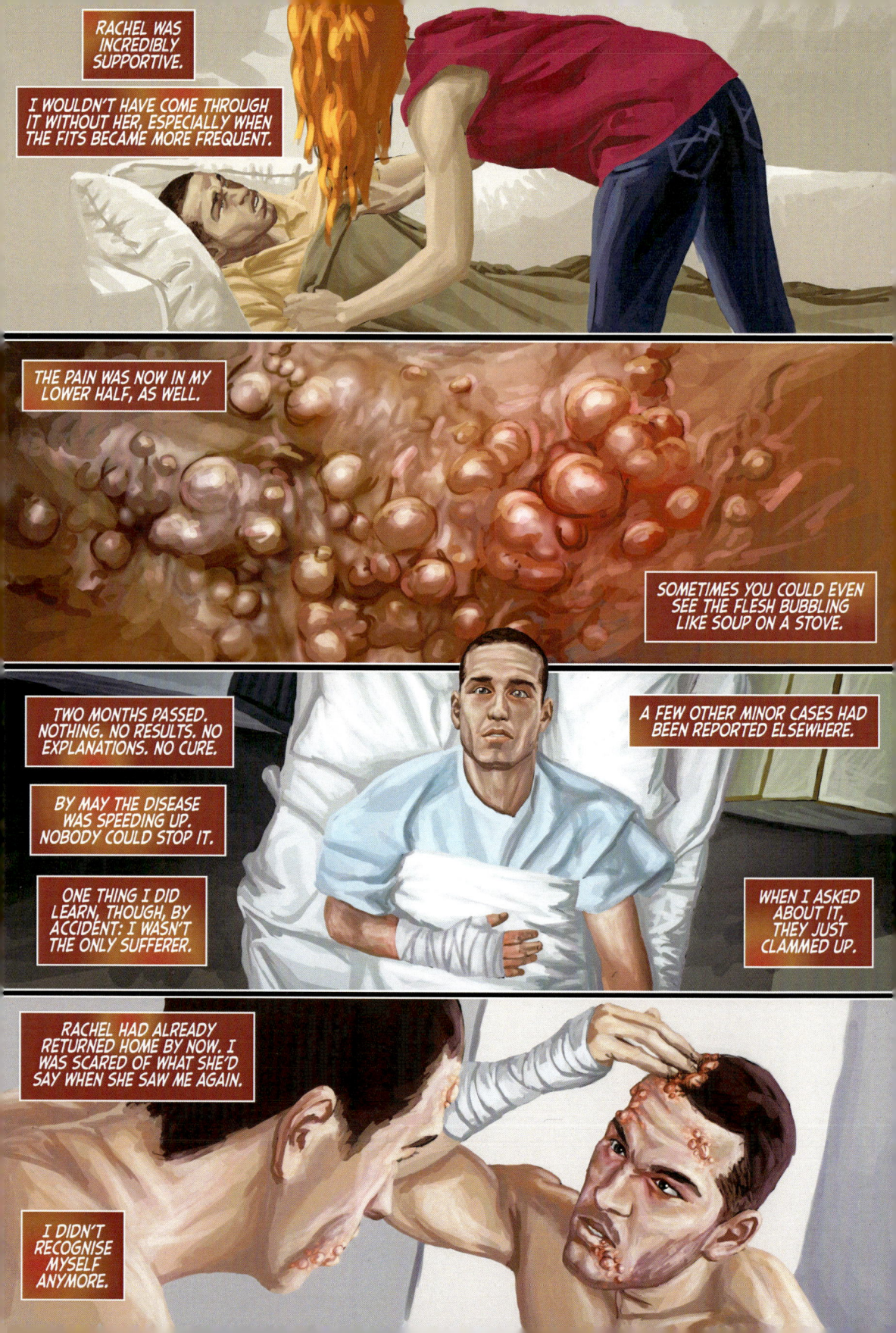

I WOULDN'T HAVE COME THROUGH IT WITHOUT HER, ESPECIALLY WHEN THE FITS BECAME MORE FREQUENT.

THE PAIN WAS NOW IN MY LOWER HALF, AS WELL.

SOMETIMES YOU COULD EVEN SEE THE FLESH BUBBLING LIKE SOUP ON A STOVE.

TWO MONTHS PASSED. NOTHING. NO RESULTS. NO EXPLANATIONS. NO CURE.

BY MAY THE DISEASE WAS SPEEDING UP. NOBODY COULD STOP IT.

ONE THING I DID LEARN, THOUGH, BY ACCIDENT: I WASN'T THE ONLY SUFFERER.

A FEW OTHER MINOR CASES HAD BEEN REPORTED ELSEWHERE.

WHEN I ASKED ABOUT IT, THEY JUST CLAMMED UP.

RACHEL HAD ALREADY RETURNED HOME BY NOW. I WAS SCARED OF WHAT SHE'D SAY WHEN SHE SAW ME AGAIN.

I DIDN'T RECOGNISE MYSELF ANYMORE.

I NEEDED A STICK. NOT EVEN THE STRONGEST MEDICATION COULD EASE THE PAIN IN MY LEGS.
RACHEL'S REACTION? A COMBINATION OF HORROR AND PITY.
THEY STILL DON'T KNOW...?
I DON'T THINK THEY EVER WILL.
IT WON'T BE MUCH USE TO ME SOON ANYWAY.
THEY HAD THEIR THEORIES: A GENETIC DISORDER, MUTATED CANCER, A REVERSAL OF F.O.P. WHICH TURNS YOUR MUSCLES INTO BONE.
NONE OF IT HELPED ME.
RACHEL SURPRISED ME THEN.
I FOUGHT BACK THE AGONY, IGNORING THE PAIN JUST TO BE NEAR HER.
THIS MUST BE WHAT IT WAS LIKE FOR THE FIRST PERSON WHO'D DEVELOPED TB, POLIO... AIDS.
KNOWING THAT NOTHING CAN BE DONE IS HARD TO TAKE.
I HAD NO ILLUSIONS. I KNEW THE END MIGHT COME AT ANY TIME.
AND STILL I DREAMED OF THE BLUE.

THEN SOME GOOD NEWS. THE DISEASE APPEARED TO GO INTO REMISSION.
MAYBE IT HAD RUN ITS COURSE, I TOLD MYSELF. AND LIKE A FOOL I STARTED TO BELIEVE IN MIRACLES AGAIN.
THE PROGRESS HALTED VERY SUDDENLY ONE WEEK.
AND THIS RESPITE LASTED THE WHOLE OF THE SUMMER.
THOUGH IT COULDN'T HAVE BEEN THE SUNLIGHT - I DIDN'T GO OUT MUCH ANYMORE.
THE DREAMS WENT AWAY AT THE SAME TIME.
I NEVER CONNECTED THAT BEFORE. A COINCIDENCE?
OR ANOTHER SYMPTOM?
I HAVE NO PROBLEM RECALLING THE DAY IT RETURNED, EITHER. IT WAS THE DAY THAT WAR WAS ANNOUNCED OVERSEAS.
THE BUILD UP TO BOTH WAS SWIFT.
A SHOCKWAVE THROUGH MY ENTIRE BODY.
AND I THOUGHT THEN...
...WHAT IF OUR ENEMIES HAD USED A CHEMICAL WEAPON ON US?
IF SO, WHY ME?
I WAS NOBODY.
RACHEL FOUND ME THERE SOME TIME LATER.

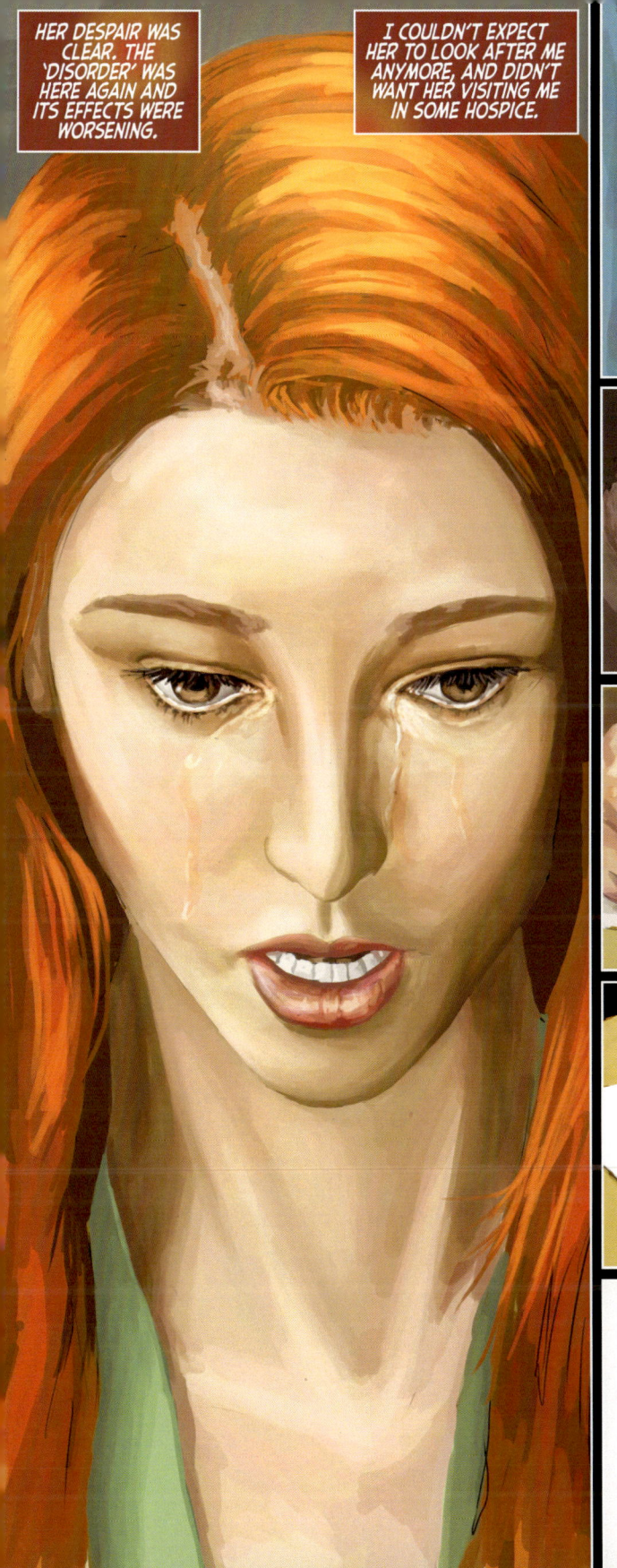

HER DESPAIR WAS CLEAR. THE 'DISORDER' WAS HERE AGAIN AND ITS EFFECTS WERE WORSENING.

I COULDN'T EXPECT HER TO LOOK AFTER ME ANYMORE, AND DIDN'T WANT HER VISITING ME IN SOME HOSPICE.

I MADE MY DECISION. I HAD TO GO.

SO THE VERY NEXT WEEK – EARLY SEPTEMBER – I WAITED FOR RACHEL TO GO OUT.

THEN I LEFT. FOR GOOD.

I THOUGHT I WAS FREEING HER. I'D BEEN A BURDEN LONG ENOUGH.

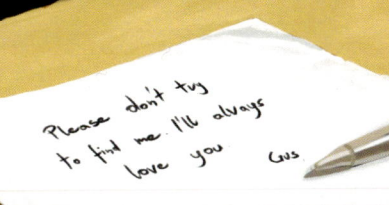

SHE LOVED ME, BUT TO STAY WOULD ONLY CAUSE HER MORE HEARTACHE.

SHE WOULD BE BETTER OFF WITHOUT ME. I SAID AS MUCH IN MY LETTER.

Please don't try to find me. I'll always love you.

Gus

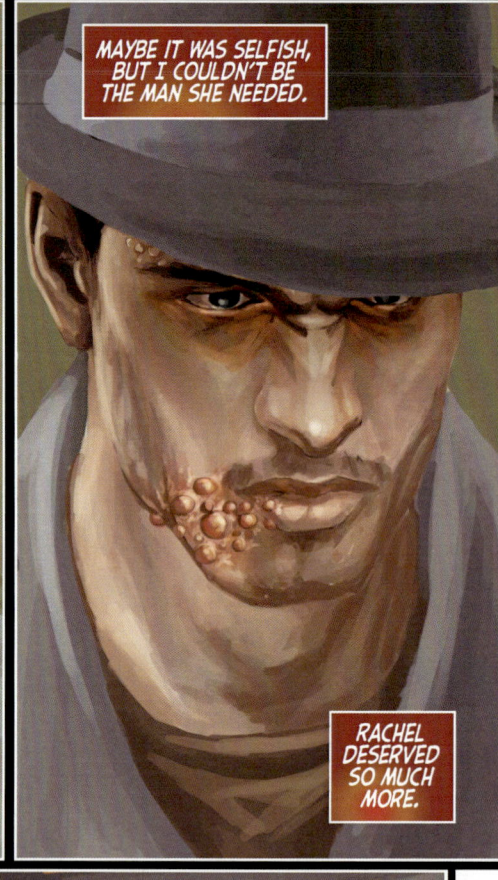

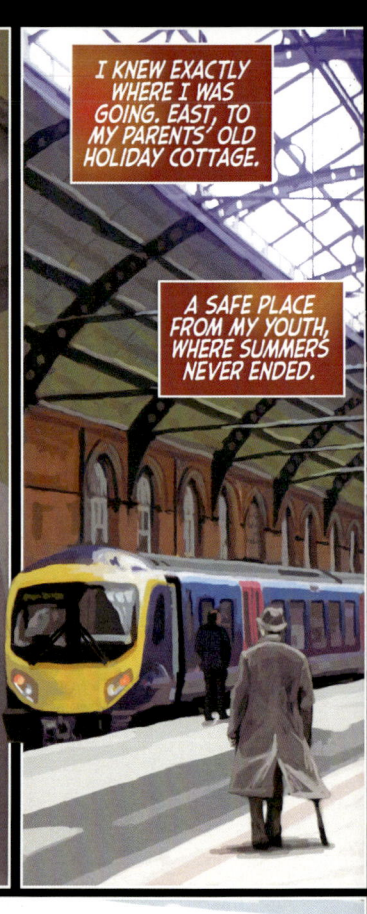

MAYBE IT WAS SELFISH, BUT I COULDN'T BE THE MAN SHE NEEDED.

REALLY, I DIDN'T KNOW WHAT I WAS DOING.

I WAS SO TERRIFIED OF BEING WITHOUT HER, YET SCARED TO BE WITH HER.

RACHEL DESERVED SO MUCH MORE.

I KNEW EXACTLY WHERE I WAS GOING. EAST, TO MY PARENTS' OLD HOLIDAY COTTAGE.

A SAFE PLACE FROM MY YOUTH, WHERE SUMMERS NEVER ENDED.

I CLIMBED ON THE TRAIN WITH GREAT DIFFICULTY.

I FELT MORE AND MORE LIKE A MONSTER WITH EACH PASSING SECOND.

FELLOW TRAVELLERS STARED AT ME, PEOPLE BACKED AWAY WHEN I GOT OFF.

THE COTTAGE SUITED ME PERFECTLY.

THE TOURIST SEASON WAS VIRTUALLY OVER, LEAVING THE NEARBY COASTAL VILLAGE EMPTY AND SAD.

I WAS HOME.
IT WAS JUST AS I REMEMBERED IT. A LITTLE MORE RUN DOWN, SURE, BUT IT WAS PEACEFUL NEAR THE SEA.
I STOCKED UP ON PROVISIONS...
DELIVERED RIGHT TO MY DOOR.
AND I SETTLED IN TO WAIT.
THE RADIO KEPT ME IN TOUCH WITH EVENTS.
OUR TROOPS ARE NOW ADVANCING ON THE FRONT LINES...
SOME ARGUED NECESSITY, OTHERS SAID THE END WAS NIGH AND THE HORSEMEN WERE SADDLING UP.
THEN ONE DAY I HEARD A PIECE ABOUT THE DISEASE.
MY DISEASE!
MORE CASES HAD BEEN DOCUMENTED IN THE LAST FEW MONTHS, FROM ALL OVER THE GLOBE.
DOCTORS WERE STARTING TO TAKE NOTICE, BUT STATED THE RISK OF CONTRACTING IT WAS MINIMAL.

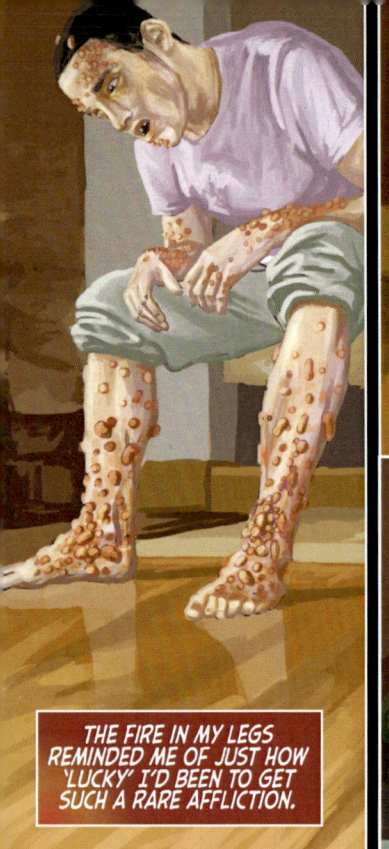

NOT LONG AFTERWARDS, I LOST THE USE OF THEM COMPLETELY.

EATING WAS A BITCH; THE LUMPS NOW INSIDE MY MOUTH AS WELL.

THE FIRE IN MY LEGS REMINDED ME OF JUST HOW 'LUCKY' I'D BEEN TO GET SUCH A RARE AFFLICTION.

SOME DAYS I DIDN'T GET UP AT ALL.

WHY SHOULD I?

I'D SMASHED ALL THE MIRRORS IN THAT COTTAGE.

HOW MUCH MORE BAD LUCK COULD IT BRING?

BUT EVERY NOW AND AGAIN THE WINDOWS WORKED AGAINST ME.

OR THE GLASS PANELLING ON THE DOOR.

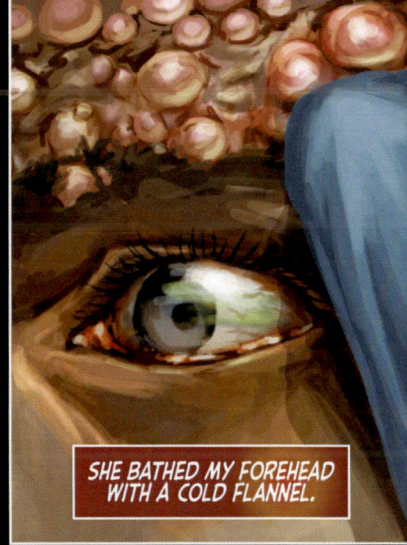

THE TEMPERATURE WAS DROPPING RAPIDLY DAY BY DAY.

YET I WAS BOILING HOT. I RAN A FEVER.

I SAW VISIONS. DELIRIOUS, I RECOGNISED OLD FAMILIAR FACES: JENKINS, FILLIS...

MY DEAD PARENTS... DAD WITH HIS ARTHRITIC HANDS...

AND RACHEL.

EXCEPT THE LAST ONE WAS REAL.

SHE TOLD ME SHE'D FINALLY FOUND THIS ADDRESS AT HOME.

SHE BATHED MY FOREHEAD WITH A COLD FLANNEL.

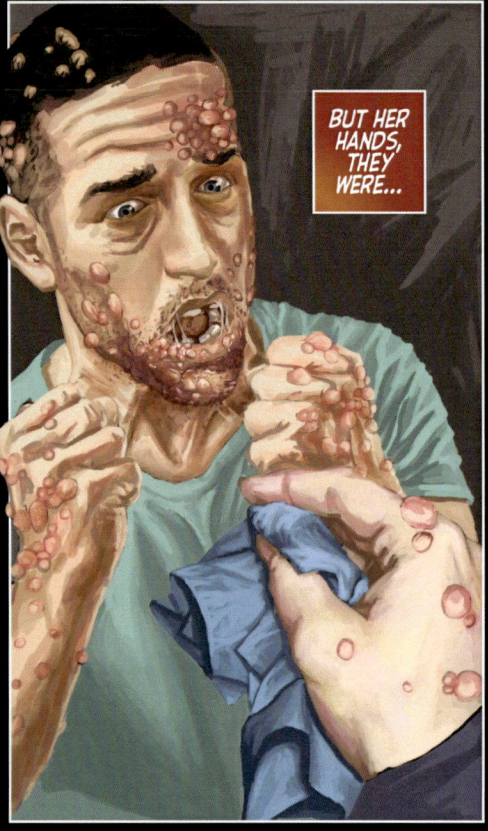

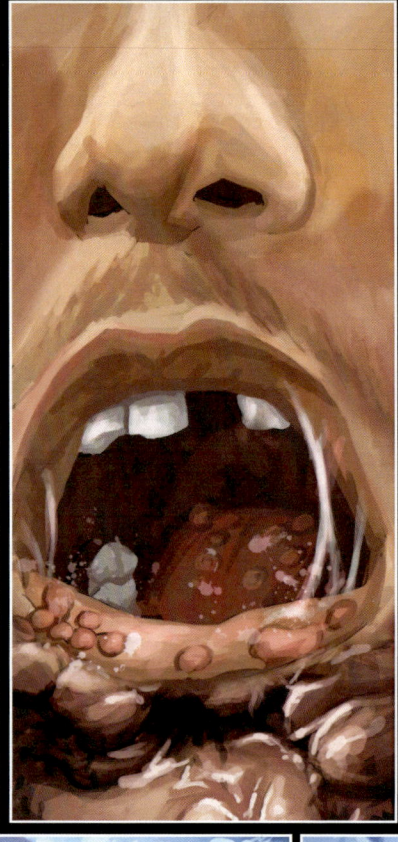

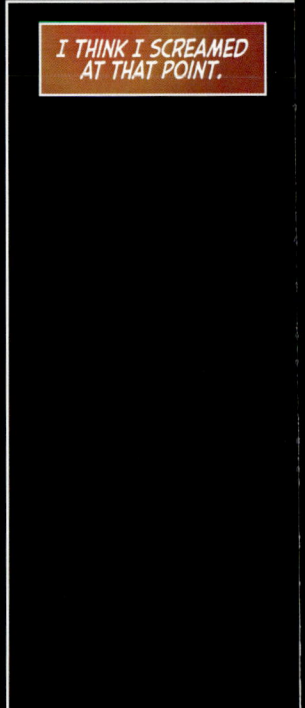

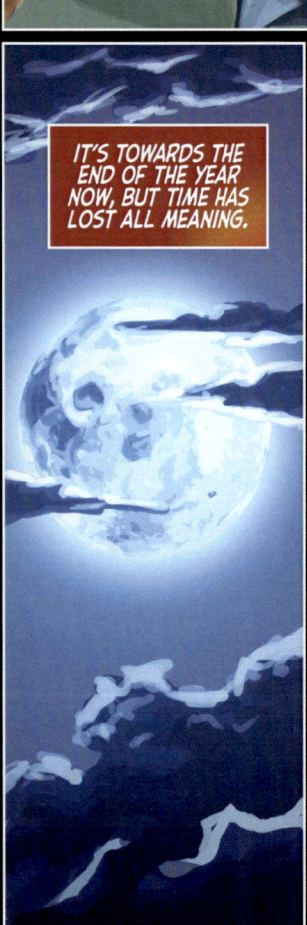

BUT HER HANDS, THEY WERE...

I THINK I SCREAMED AT THAT POINT.

IT'S TOWARDS THE END OF THE YEAR NOW, BUT TIME HAS LOST ALL MEANING.

RACHEL SAID THE WAR WAS OVER. NO ONE GIVES A SHIT ABOUT FIGHTING ANYMORE.

MILLIONS HAVE THE DISEASE. THE PLAGUE IS UNCONTROLLABLE, UNPREDICTABLE. UNSTOPPABLE.

IT HAPPENED MUCH MORE QUICKLY FOR RACHEL THAN ME.

THE PAIN MUCH GREATER.

ALL I COULD DO WAS BE THERE FOR HER.

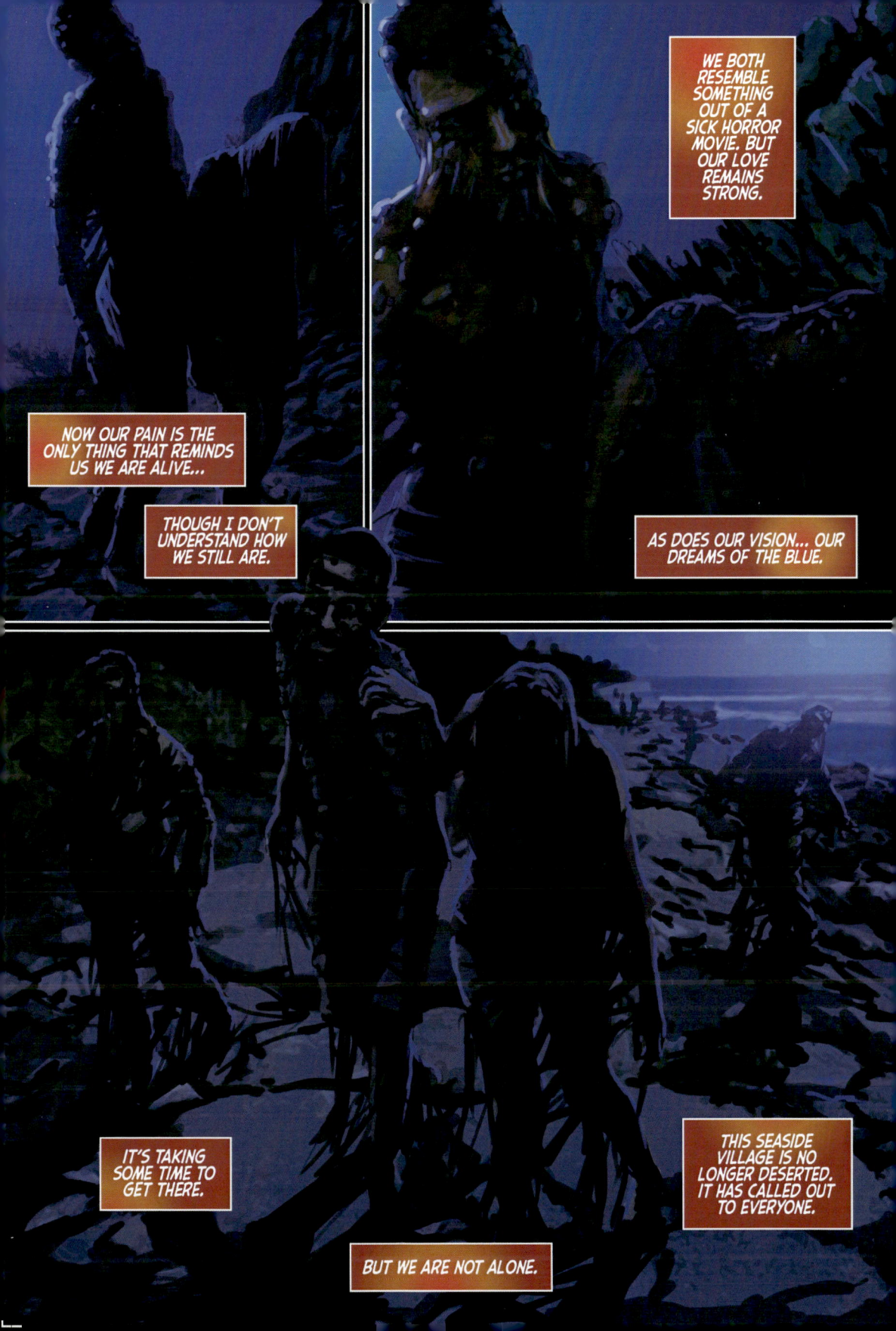

NOW OUR PAIN IS THE ONLY THING THAT REMINDS US WE ARE ALIVE...

THOUGH I DON'T UNDERSTAND HOW WE STILL ARE.

WE BOTH RESEMBLE SOMETHING OUT OF A SICK HORROR MOVIE. BUT OUR LOVE REMAINS STRONG.

AS DOES OUR VISION... OUR DREAMS OF THE BLUE.

IT'S TAKING SOME TIME TO GET THERE.

THIS SEASIDE VILLAGE IS NO LONGER DESERTED. IT HAS CALLED OUT TO EVERYONE.

BUT WE ARE NOT ALONE.

THE BEACH IS FULL OF QUIVERING SHAPES THAT USED TO BE...WELL, US. AND EVEN, YES EVEN THOSE WHO HAVE NOT YET UNDERGONE THE TRANSFORMATION BY THIS LATE STAGE. THEIR BLOODCURDLING CRIES CAN BE HEARD FOR MILES AROUND.

IN MY IMAGINATION, I SEE SCENES LIKE THESE OCCURRING ALL OVER THE COUNTRY. ALL AROUND THE WORLD...

WE'VE TALKED IT OVER AND THINK WE KNOW WHY NOW.

WHY WE ARE RETURNING TO WHAT WE ONCE WERE.

AND AS RACHEL AND I JOIN AGAIN, GLIDING OVER THE TIDE, OUR SUSPICIONS ARE CONFIRMED.

WE ARE THE DISEASE.

ALL OF US.

IT'S TAKEN SOME DOING, BUT OUR PLANET HAS AT LAST FOUND A CURE - SOME MIGHT SAY JUST IN TIME!

HARD TO THINK CLEARLY... BUT... THERE IS NO REASON TO FIGHT IT NOW. THIS ISN'T SO BAD.

JUST EXISTENCE, AND THE PROMISE OF ETERNITY.

ITS ANTIBODIES HAVE BEEN ATTACKING US INVISIBLY IN THE AIR, IN OUR FOOD, IN THE WATER... REVERSING MILLIONS OF YEARS OF EVOLUTION.

BECOMING ONE WITH THE LIQUID, WITH EACH OTHER. NO WORRIES, NO ANXIETY, NO HARDSHIP. NO WAR.

AT LEAST FOR NOW.

AT LEAST FOR...

THE END

… SHOCK VALUE presents

THE DISEASE

Hellbound Media wish to thank the following people for all their support in bringing this project to life. Thanks for making our Kickstarter a success!

Stefan Hamann	Matthew Brown
Deadstar Publishing	Jonathan Kui
Stuart Gould	Nick Ashby
Steve Tanner	John A. Short
Shaun Hastings	Stefan Simovic
Victor Wright – Geeky Comics	Joyce Ann Garcia
Esther Mullings	Robert Flores
Erik Hofstatter	Haley McDonald
Jenny Ashcroft	Slocko Flyde Coast Comics
Winston Kou	Karl Andrews
James Nettles	Arthur Digby Sellers
Mika Koyyka	Omar Pineda
Mark Hetherington	kurokun
Jean-Luc Reyes	Neil Ashworth
JordanCookFILMS	Daniel Farrand
Simon Blanchett-Parker	Ant O'Reilly
James Azrael / The HSPPA	Fifth Dimension Comics
Reed Andrus	Tom Spellman
Anthony Bagley	Matt Warner
Maz Johnson	Jake Shellenberger
James McCulloch	Peter Raber
Helen Brannigan	Andrew Lee
Curtis Smith	Lukasz Michalski
Comichaus	Richard Anderson
Dennis Strasburg	Pippa Bailey
Jon Radigan	Derogan

PRINTED BY UK COMICS
EST. 2005

www.ukcomicscreative.co.uk

GAME BOARDS · FLYERS · STICKER ALBUMS · BAGS · CANVAS PRINTS · COMICS · DISPLAY BOARDS · T SHIRTS · GLICEE PRINTS · VEHICLE GRAPHICS · VINYL GRAPHICS · PACKAGING · HARD COVERS · STATIONERY · PULL UP BANNERS · BROCHURES · PAPERBACKS · BADGES · GAME SETS · LEAFLETS · LANYARDS

THE CLOWNED PRINTS OF COMICS

WWW.UKCOMICSCREATIVE.CO.UK

STUART@UKCOMICSCREATIVE.CO.UK E: HAI@UKONDISPLAY.COM T: 01793 766766

DEADSTAR PUBLISHING

Comics ★ Graphic Novels ★ Books

DEXTER'S HALF DOZEN
By Jamie Lambert and Dave Clifford

High adventure and horror beyond imagination await in this thrilling cult comic series! December, 1941. Sergeant Freeman of the newly formed S.A.S. is seconded by Sir Dexter Kilby - Churchill's occult adviser - to lead a ragtag band of criminals and misfits behind enemy lines in an ongoing war against Nazi occult forces. Suggested for mature readers.

THACKERAY: NOT QUITE DEAD
By Joanne Chong and Kris Wozencroft

Thackeray has a secret - can he keep it? It's 2013 and the zombie apocalypse has been and gone. Now Abel Thackeray is part of the team that cleans up the last few undead stragglers. There's just one problem... He has a wound on his arm that won't heal and a constant hunger for flesh.

RISING STARS: VOLUME #2
By various up and coming new talent!

Coming Soon!
Gourmet demons, machiavellian masterminds and more... Showcasing fantastic new creators, the Rising Stars: Volume 2 anthology continues our tradition of searching out exciting stories from little-known gifted writers and artists and delivering them slice by slice to our fans. Volume 1 started careers - Volume 2 will do the same!

www.deadstarpublishing.co.uk

f /deadstar.publishing   **t** @DSPublishing